Q W L Y H R C E F U N V S

The Little
Red Cat
Who Ran Away
and Learned His
A·B·C's
(the Hard Way)

PATRICK McDONNELL

LITTLE, BROWN AND COMPANY
NEW YORK   BOSTON

Little, Brown and Company

Hachette Book Group
1290 Avenue of the Americas, New York, NY 10104
Visit us at lb-kids.com

Little, Brown and Company is a division of Hachette Book Group, Inc.
The Little, Brown name and logo are trademarks of Hachette Book Group, Inc.

The publisher is not responsible for websites (or their content) that are not owned by the publisher.

First Edition: September 2017

Library of Congress Cataloging-in-Publication Data
Names: McDonnell, Patrick, 1956– author, illustrator.
Title: The little red cat : (who ran away from home and learned his ABC's the hard way) / Patrick McDonnell.
Description: First edition. | New York : Little, Brown and Company Books for Young Readers, 2017. | Summary: "In this nearly wordless alphabet book, a little red cat runs away and gets caught up in a wild chase that goes everywhere from A to Z and back home again"— Provided by publisher.
Identifiers: LCCN 2016033555| ISBN 9780316502467 (hardcover : alk. paper) | ISBN 9780316502474 (e-book : alk. paper)
Subjects: | CYAC: Cats—Fiction. | Alphabet.
Classification: LCC PZ7.M1554 Li 2017 | DDC [E]—dc23
LC record available at https://lccn.loc.gov/2016033555

10 9 8 7 6 5 4 3 2 1

APS

ISBNs: 978-0-316-50246-7 (hardcover), 978-0-316-50247-4 (ebook), 978-0-316-51076-9 (ebook), 978-0-316-51075-2 (ebook)

PRINTED IN CHINA

This book was edited by Andrea Spooner and designed by Jeff Schulz and Patrick McDonnell with art direction by Jen Keenan. The production was supervised by Erika Schwartz, and the production editor was Annie McDonnell. The illustrations for this book were done in pen and ink, pencil, and watercolor, with spot digital color. The text was set in Merriweather, and the display type is Didot.

Aa

Bb

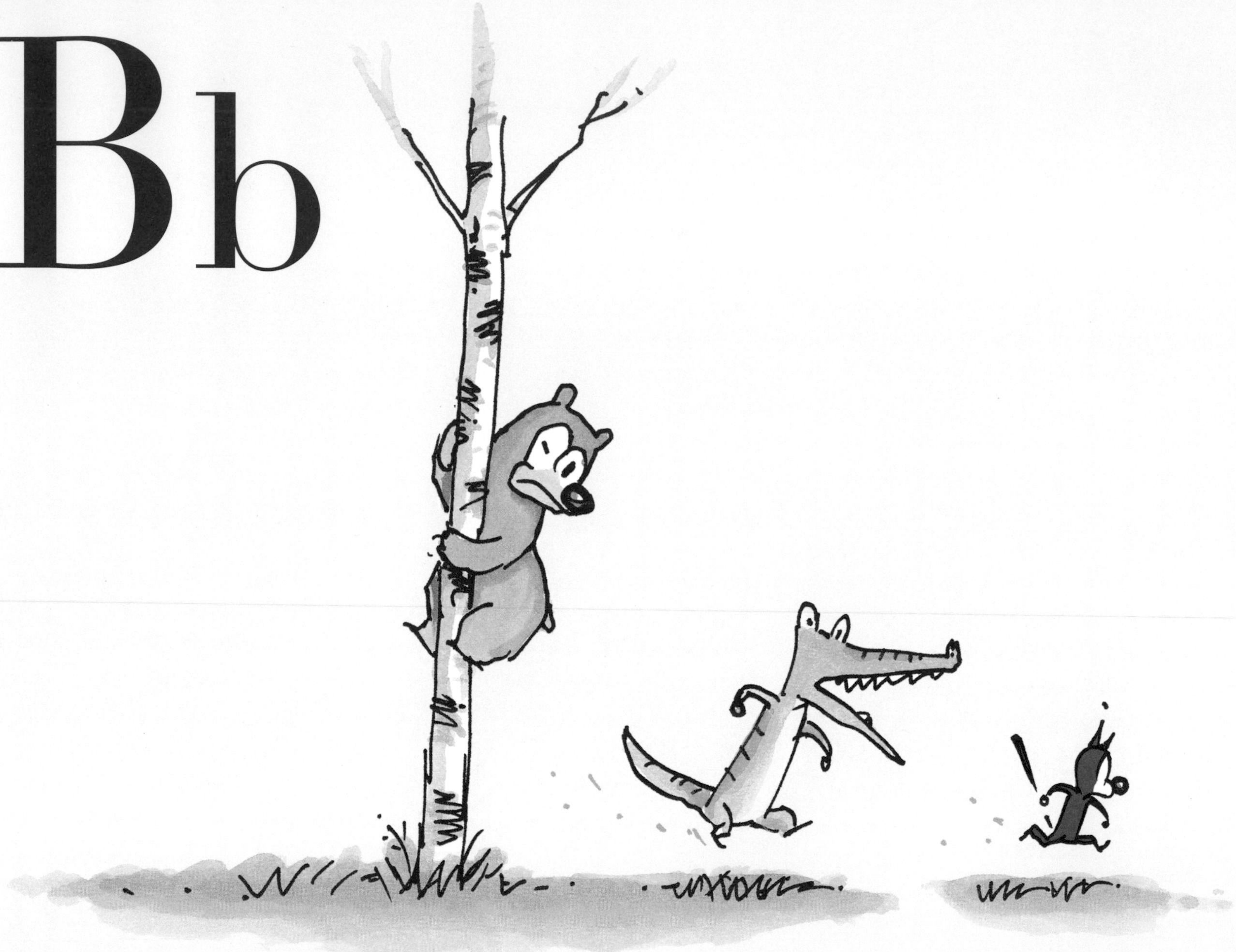

Cc

Dd

Ee

Ff

Gg

Hh

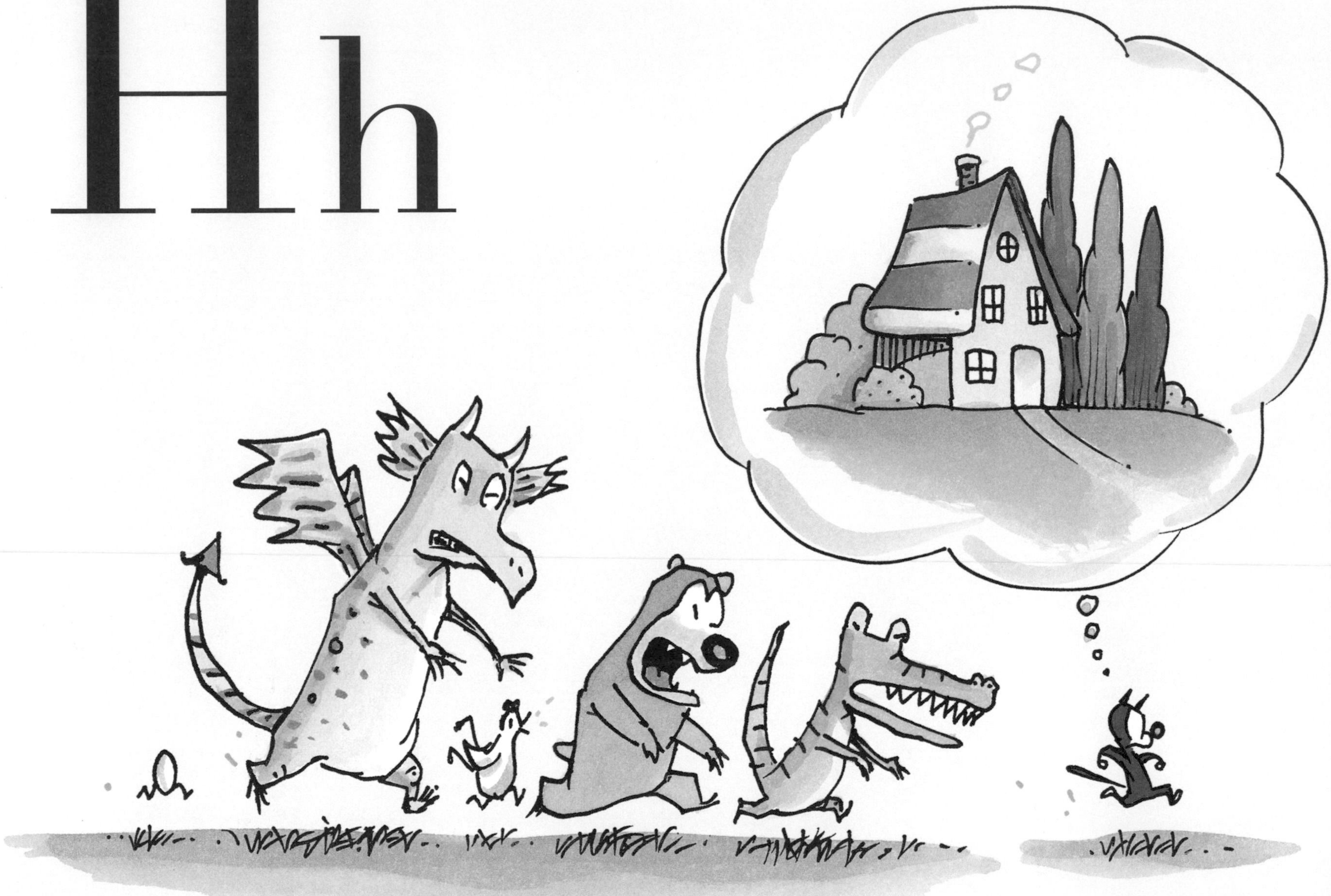

Ii

Jj

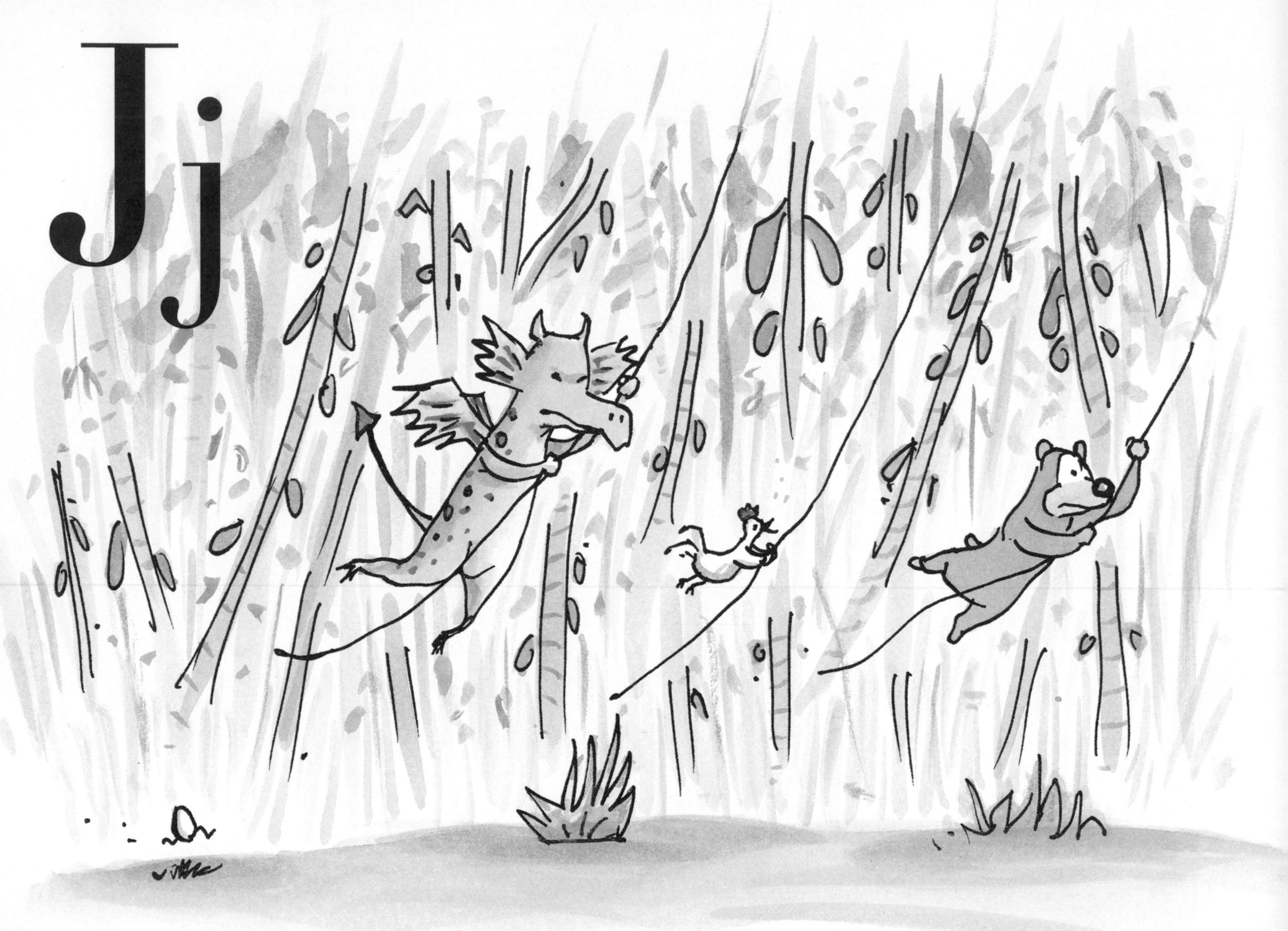

K k

Mm

Nnnnnnn

Oooooooo!

Qq

Rr

S s

T t

Uu

Vv

Ww

Xx

Y y

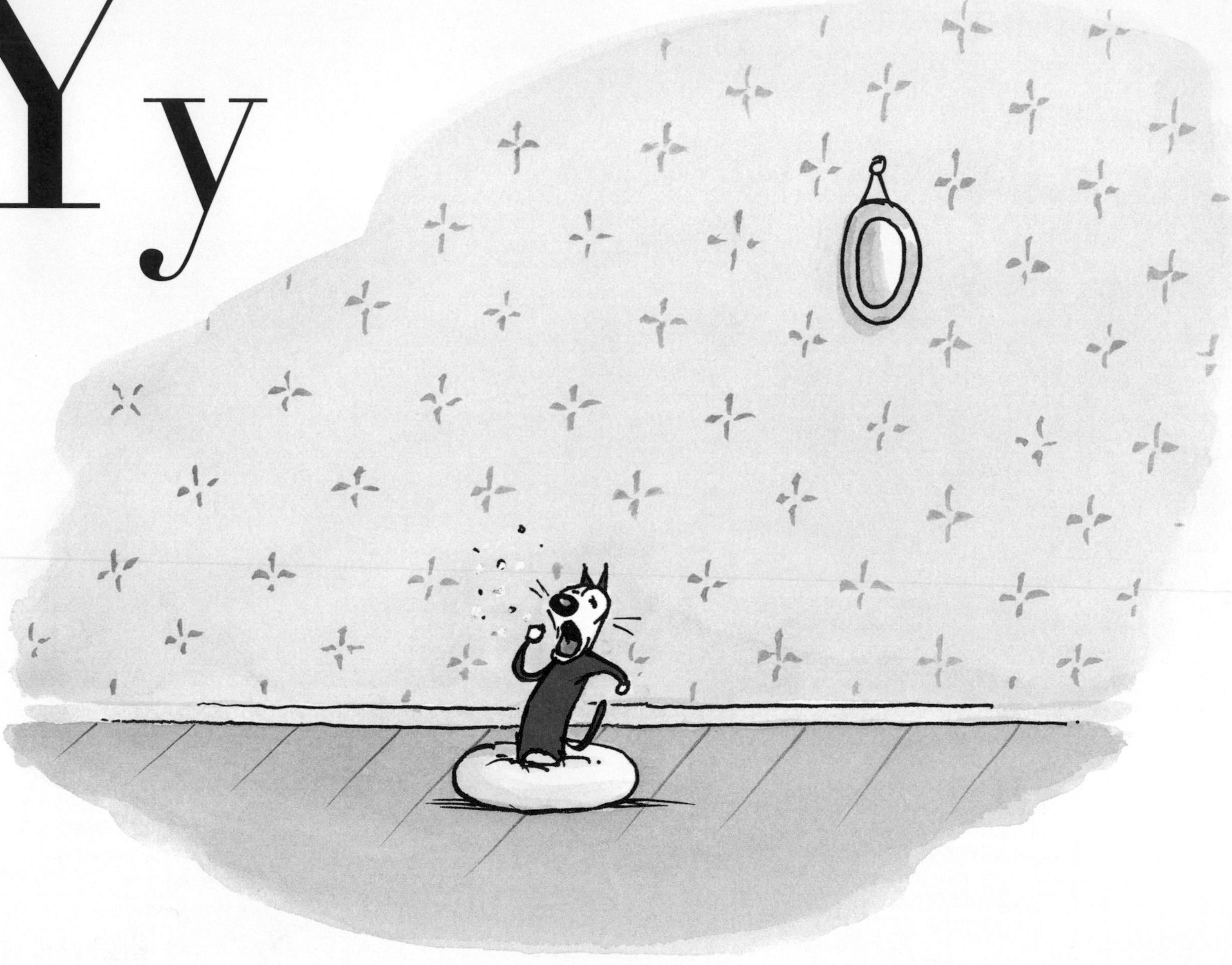

A – alligator   **F** – fire   **K** – king   **P** – parachute   **U** – unicorn

B – bear   **G** – glasses   **L** – lost   **Q** – questions   **V** – valentine

C – chicken   **H** – home/house   **M** – mountains   **R** – restroom   **W** – wave

D – dragon   **I** – ice   **N** – no   **S** – sunset   **X** – x marks the spot

E – egg   **J** – jungle   **O** – over   **T** – tired   **Y** – yawn

                                                                                            Z – zzz

D J A M
O T Z X
G I
K P B